# RUMPELSTILTSKIN

*To Jackie Mattoon*

Copyright © 1985 by Paul Galdone

All rights reserved. Published in the United States by HMH Books, an imprint of Houghton Mifflin Harcourt Publishing Company. Originally published in hardcover in the United States by Clarion Books, an imprint of Houghton Mifflin Harcourt Publishing Company, 1985.

For information about permission to reproduce selections from this book, write to Permissions, Houghton Mifflin Harcourt Publishing Company, 215 Park Avenue South, New York, New York 10003.

www.hmhbooks.com

The Library of Congress Cataloging-in-Publication data is on file.

ISBN: 978-0-89919-266-6 hardcover
ISBN: 978-0-395-52599-9 paperback
ISBN: 978-0-547-18181-3 book and CD
ISBN: 978-0-544-06692-2 paper over board

Manufactured in China
SCP 10 9 8 7 6 5 4 3 2 1
4500418311

*Retold and Illustrated by*

# PAUL GALDONE

# STILTSKIN

## A FOLK TALE CLASSIC

Houghton Mifflin Harcourt
Boston   New York

Once upon a time there was a poor miller whose
only treasure was his beautiful daughter.

Now it happened that the miller had to go on an errand to the King. The miller wanted to make himself appear important, so he said: "I have a daughter who can spin straw into gold."

"That is a marvelous art," replied the King. "If your daughter is as clever as you say, bring her to my palace tomorrow and I will put her to a test."

When the King said that, the miller regretted his boast. But he knew he must obey the King's command.

As soon as the miller's daughter arrived at the palace, the King took her into a room which was full of straw. He gave her a spinning wheel and some bobbins and said: "Now set to work. And if by dawn tomorrow you have not spun this straw into gold, you must die."

He locked the door, and left the miller's daughter alone in the room. There she sat, for she had no idea how straw could be spun into gold. As the hours passed, she grew more and more frightened. At last she began to weep.

All at once the door opened and in came a little man. "Good evening," he said. "Why are you crying so?"

"Alas!" answered the girl. "I have to spin straw into gold, and I do not know how to do it."

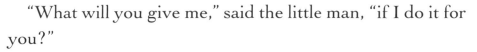

"What will you give me," said the little man, "if I do it for you?"

"My necklace," said the girl.

The little man took the necklace and seated himself in front of the wheel. *Whirr, whirr, whirr,* it went, and in three turns the bobbin was full.

He put on another and *whirr, whirr, whirr,* the second bobbin was full, too. And so it went until dawn, when all the straw was spun, and all the bobbins were full of gold. Then the little man slipped out the door.

When the King arrived and saw the gold, he was astonished and delighted. But his heart only became more greedy.

He had the miller's daughter taken into a larger room, which was also full of straw. "If you value your life," he said, "you must spin this straw into gold by dawn tomorrow."

The miller's daughter looked at the pile of straw and began to cry. Just then the door opened and the little man appeared again.

"What will you give me," said the little man, "if I spin this straw into gold for you?"

"The ring on my finger," answered the girl.

The little man took the ring, and began to turn the wheel again. By next morning he had spun all the straw into glittering gold.

The King rejoiced at the sight, but still he was not satisfied.

He had the miller's daughter taken into an even larger room full of straw, and he said: "You must spin this, too, in the course of a night. And if you succeed, you shall be my wife."

As he locked the door, he thought: "She may only be a miller's daughter, but I am sure I could not find a richer wife in the whole world."

When the girl was alone, the little man came for the third time and said: "What will you give me if I spin this straw for you also?"

"I have nothing of value left," said the girl.

"Then promise me, if you should become Queen, to give me your first child."

"Who knows whether that will ever happen?" thought the miller's daughter. So, not knowing how else to help herself, she promised to give the little man what he wanted.

Grinning, he sat down at the wheel and once more spun the straw into gold.

When the King came in the morning and saw all that gold, he arranged a grand marriage, and the beautiful miller's daughter became Queen.

A year later, the Queen gave birth to a beautiful baby daughter. She was so happy with the child that she never once thought about the little man. But one day he suddenly appeared in her room and said, "Now give me what you promised."

The Queen was horrified and offered the little man all the riches of the kingdom if he would let her keep the child.

But the little man said, "No. Something alive is dearer to me than all the treasures in the world."

At that the Queen began to sob so loudly that the little man took pity on her. "I will give you three days," he said. "If by the end of that time you find out my name, then you shall keep your child."

The Queen stayed up the whole night, thinking of all the names she had ever heard, and she sent a messenger out to search far and wide for other names.

When the little man came to the palace the next day, the Queen began with Caspar, Melchior, and Balthazar, and then said all the names she knew, one after the other. But to each one the little man said, "That is not my name."

On the second day, the Queen learned the names of everyone living near the palace. When the little man came again, she selected the most unusual ones. "Perhaps your name is Shortribs," she said, "or Sheepshanks, or Lace-leg?"

But the little man always answered: "That is not my name."

On the third day the messenger returned, and told the Queen: "I have not been able to find a single new name. But as I approached a high mountain at the end of the forest, I saw a little house.

"Before the house a fire was burning, and round about the fire a little man was jumping. He hopped first on one leg and then the other, and shouted:

'Today I brew, tomorrow I bake.
The next day, the young Queen's child I'll take.
Soon far and wide will spread the fame
That Rumpelstiltskin is my name.'"

How glad the Queen was when she heard the messenger's story. She repeated the name Rumpelstiltskin over and over.

Soon afterward the little man came in and asked: "Now, Queen, what is my name?"

At first she said, "Is it Conrad?"

"No."

"Is it Harry?"

"No."

"Then perhaps your name is Rumpelstiltskin?"

"The devil told you that! The devil told you that!" cried the little man.

In his rage, he stamped his right foot on the ground so hard that he sank to his waist. Then he stamped his left foot so hard that he disappeared from sight.

The earth fell in on top of him,
and Rumpelstiltskin
was never seen again.

THE END

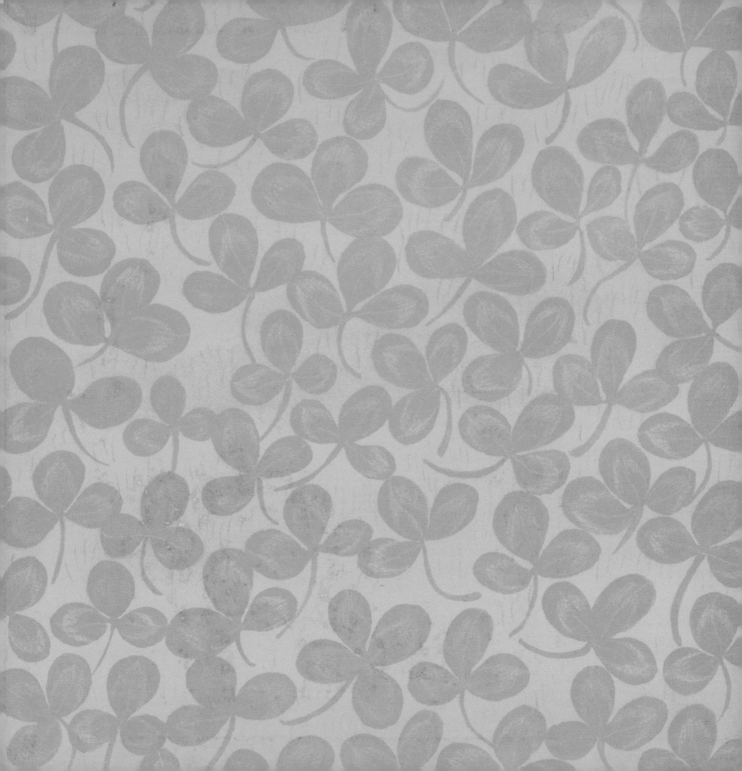